Swollobog

Alastair Taylor

Houghton Mifflin Company
Boston 2001

For MiniMum (belatedly)
and the Bean

All rights reserved. For information about permission
to reproduce selections from this book, write to
Permissions, Houghton Mifflin Company,
215 Park Avenue South, New York, New York 10003.

www.houghtonmifflinbooks.com

The text of this book is set in Adobe Nueva MM.
The illustrations are acrylics.

Library of Congress Cataloging-in-Publication Data

Taylor, Alastair.
Swollobog / Alastair Taylor.
p. cm.
Summary: On an outing to the fair, a perpetually hungry little dog
swallows a helium balloon and leads his owners on a wild chase.
ISBN 0-618-04348-9
[1. Dogs — Fiction. 2. Humorous stories.] I. Title.
PZ7.T211575 Sw 2001
[E] — dc 21   00-033610

Manufactured in the United States of America
WOZ 10 9 8 7 6 5 4 3 2 1

One day a little girl was practicing her letters. She wanted to write the name of her dog, who was always swallowing things, but she wrote the *d* backward. Her dog has been known as Swollobog ever since.

She spelled *swallow* wrong too, but she was very young.

The little girl is me. I'm Meg. Hello.

And this is Swollobog.

Now I know Swollobog is a silly name for a dog, but if I tell you
about her, I think you'll understand.

It's really all a matter of GREEDINESS. . . .

She was always a bit impatient for her dinner and would find ways of reminding us when it was time. She usually picked on Dad because he's such a softie.

Then she would make sure he appreciated just how HUNGRY she really was.

When she got her food, it disappeared more and more quickly each day as she bothered less and less with things like chewing and breathing. Then one day she ate so fast she swallowed it all in one gulp—bowl included.

You might think that's as greedy as a small dog could get.

You'd be wrong.

If someone thinks of popping into the kitchen for a snack ...

Swollobog will usually be there first with a kind of "me too" expression on her face. She can smell the thought of cheese, you see.

When all hints fail (and they usually do), she just swallows anything we've forgotten to hide. Bananas, toast, and peanut brittle are her particular favorites, besides cheese. She also likes carrots, yogurt, pizza, toenail clippings, and door handles. Oh, and blueberry muffins, snails, mud, toothpaste, lemons …

I can't think where I put that sack of potatoes

Let's face it, she'll swallow anything that isn't nailed down.

She can hear two bananas rubbing together in a shopping bag two streets away, but if you go up to her and shout …

WALKIES!

she becomes awfully hard of hearing.

HEEL!

SIT!

FETCH!

STAY! hm, not bad

LEAVE!

DOWN!

FORGET IT

I'm going to have

some chocolate

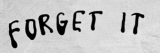

We have tried to reform her. Once I had
a great idea to teach her not to be so greedy.

I should have known better.

We also should have known better, she being the kind of dog she is, than to take her to the fair. But, well, I suppose we love her. OK, when she's just swallowed something really embarrassing we love her a little less, but we still love her, and on the day of the fair she had been good—just her usual seventeen slices of toast for breakfast and no extra swallowing on the side—so anyway, whatever the reason, whatever *POSSESSED* us, we decided to take her to the fair.

She wasn't that impressed with the bumper cars and the big
dipper—she couldn't see the point.

She brightened up when we bought her some cotton candy, but one swallow later, she couldn't understand why something so large and promising could take up so little stomach space. She enjoyed the moon walk, though, as children's candy kept falling out of their pockets.

All in all, the visit to the fair
wasn't going too badly...

until she spotted...

the balloon man.

I don't know what it was about the balloon. Perhaps she was showing off to the balloon dog.

Or perhaps the balloon man had packed his balloons next to his sandwiches and they had acquired a cheesy aroma. I don't even know how she got off her leash, although she does have an uncanny ability to shrink her head when it's really necessary.

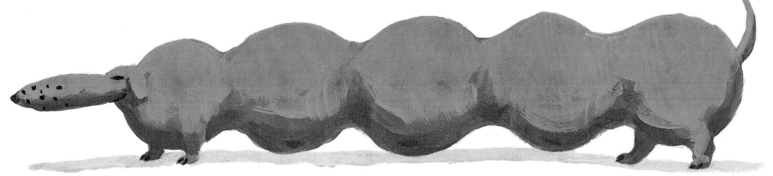

Anyway—she swallowed a balloon.
Which wouldn't have mattered all that much...

except that it was a HELIUM balloon.

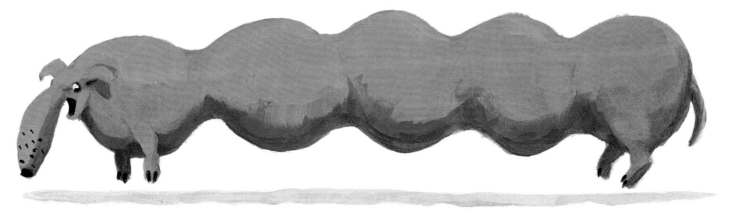

Before anyone could grab her, she floated gently out of reach.
Soon she was above the treetops and drifting away toward the
beach. Now, even if you're a bit cross with your dog, you can't just
let her float away. Besides, she was terrified of heights. You would
be too, if you had legs that short.

The trouble was, the higher she got, the more wind there was.
And the more wind there was, the faster she headed out to sea.

What are we going to do?

WAIT FOR THE BALLOON TO GO DOWN

but she'll be miles out to sea by then!

Wah!

PERHAPS THE WIND WILL CHANGE

perhaps it won't

WAH!

SO WE MUST POP THE BALLOON

but we'll pop Swollobog!

WAH!

NOT IF WE POP IT FROM THE INSIDE

??

WE HAVE TO MAKE HER SWALLOW SOMETHING SHARP!

She'll swallow anything, but...

WE NEED A HANG-GLIDING HEDGEHOG

ha!

HA!

wah?

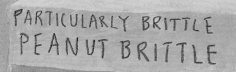

We bought the biggest, sharpest piece of peanut brittle, and a boy let us tie it to the tail of his kite. Then he launched the kite and started to let out the string.

Swollobog was just a speck in the distance.

Soon all the string was out and the boy's feet were wet, but the kite still hadn't reached Swollobog.

oops!

can I help?

CHAMPION KITE FLYER

We all got into the old fisherman's boat and he rowed out to sea as fast as he could, which wasn't all that fast. But the wind was so strong that the boy was lifted into the air. So we tied him to the seat, just to be on the safe side, and the same wind that was blowing Swollobog away helped to tow us after her.

It took a few passes to get the tail of the kite under her nose, but at last we saw through the old fisherman's binoculars…

There was a pause.

Then a muffled pop.

The boy had difficulty winding in the string, since he was tied to the seat. So Dad took over, and at last in came the kite … the tail … and no peanut brittle … and … no … Swollobog.

She had never learned to swim. It had always seemed too strenuous.

And then an idea came to us—

an idea we all had at the same moment and all thought was silly
but knew was our only hope.

It was the sort of small, wriggly idea that starts somewhere
behind the left ear and oozes forward.

We explained it to the old fisherman and the boy, and together
we all thought as hard as we could about …

Swollobog was quite annoyed about the lack of actual cheese in the boat. Luckily she had met several haddock while in the sea, and when we got back to shore we bought her six cheeseburgers to cheer her up.

She looked a bit bedraggled after her experience, and somehow a little smaller than before, but she was still our Swollobog, and we were reasonably pleased to have her back.

You probably think she gave up swallowing things after a shock like that.

NAH!

The next day she swallowed my bike.